To Nancy

IN A SPRING

Edited by Richard Lewis

Pictures by Ezra Jack Keats

GARDEN

The Dial Press   New York

A red morning sky,
For you, snail;
  Are you glad about it?
     —*Issa*

Grasshopper,
Do not trample to pieces
The pearls of bright dew.
—*Issa*

The frog
Is having a staring match
With me.

—*Issa*

The toad! It looks as if
It would belch forth
A cloud!

—*Issa*

"I've just come from a place
At the lake bottom"—that is the look
On the little duck's face.
                    —*Bashō*

A day of spring;
In the garden,
Sparrows bathing in the sand.
—*Onitsura*

The chicken
    Wants to say something,
The way it's using its feet.
        —*Anonymous*

Voices
Above the white clouds:
Skylarks.
—*Kyoroku*

A flash of lightning!
The sound of dew
Dripping down the bamboos.
—*Buson*

A drop of rain!
The frog wiped his forehead
With his wrist.
                —*Issa*

Come on, Owl!
Come on, change that look of yours
Now in the soft spring rain!

—*Issa*

Stillness:
The sound of the petals
Sifting down together.
—*Chora*

The bat
Lives hidden
Under the broken umbrella.
—*Buson*

The puppy asleep
Biting
The willow tree.
—*Issa*

Ha! the butterfly!
—it is following the person
who stole the flowers!
—*Anonymous*

Just simply alive,
Both of us, I
And the poppy.
                    —*Issa*

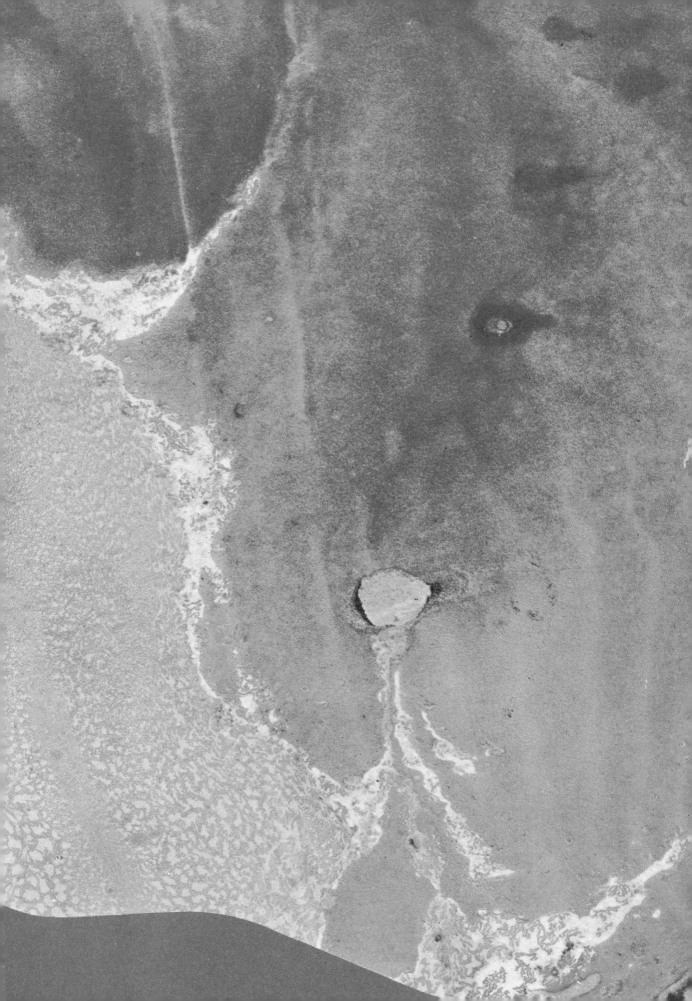

The blind sparrow
Hops on the flower
Of the evening glory.
—Gyôdai

With the evening breeze
The water laps against
The heron's legs.
—*Buson*

On how to sing
    the frog school and the skylark school
        are arguing.

                        —*Shiki*

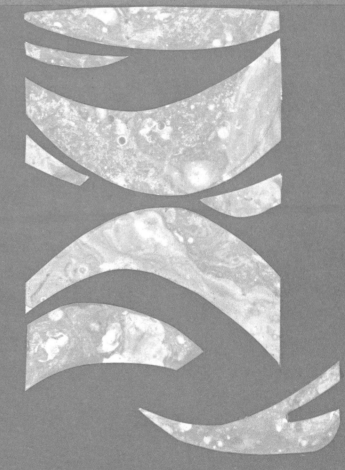

The moon in the water
Turned a somersault
And floated away.
—*Ryôta*

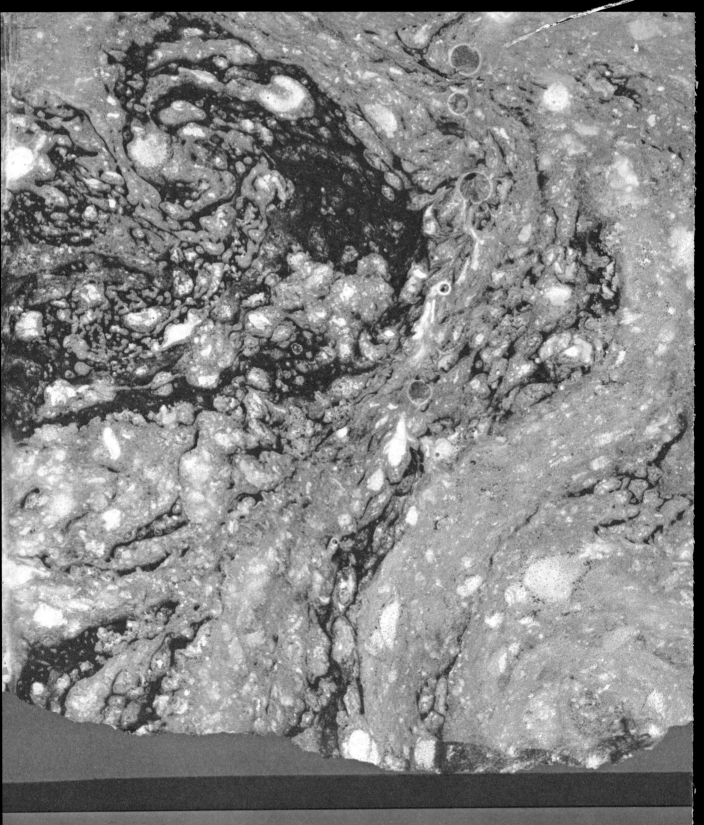

How lovely,
Through the torn paper window
The Milky Way.

—*Issa*

The nightingales sing
In the echo of the bell
Tolled at evening.
—*Ukō*

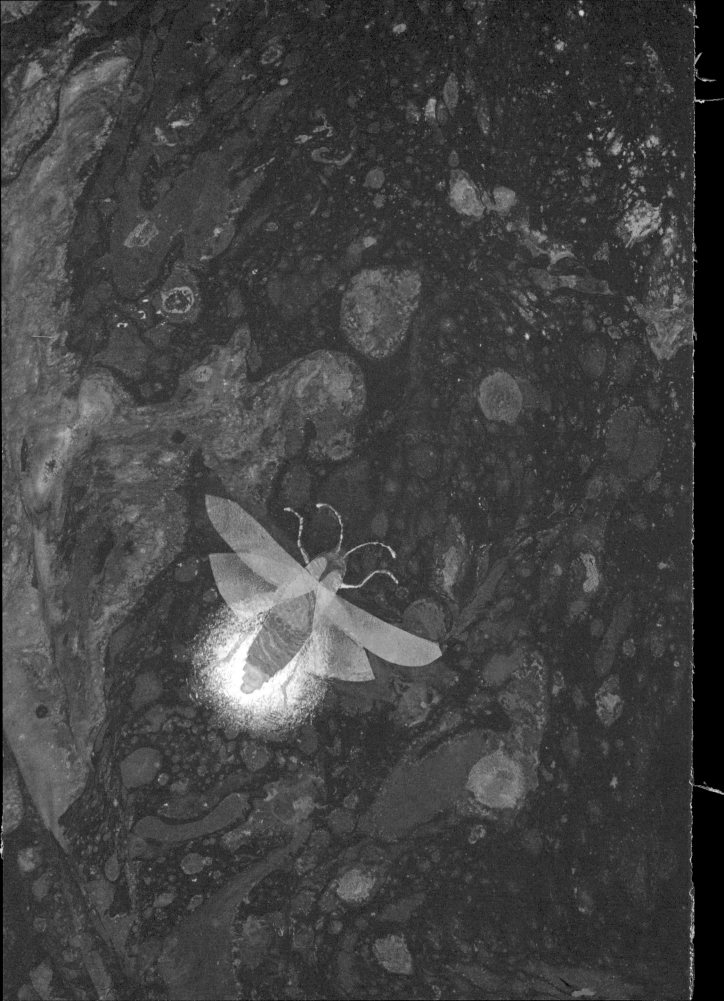

A giant firefly:
     that way, this way, that way, this—
     and it passes by.

                —Issa

Acknowledgments

The editor wishes to express his gratitude to the following publishers and authors for permission to include material in this anthology from their original publications.

"A giant firefly—" and "On how to sing—" from *An Introduction to Haiku* by Harold G. Henderson. Copyright 1958 by Harold G. Henderson. Reprinted by permission of Doubleday & Company, Inc. "A red morning sky—" "The bat—" "The blind sparrow—" "The chicken—" "A day of spring—" "A flash of lightning—" "The frog—" "Grasshopper—" "How lovely—" " 'I've just come—' " "Just simply alive—" "The moon—" "The puppy asleep—" "Stillness—" "The toad—" "Voices—" and "With the evening breeze—" from *Haiku,* edited and translated by R. H. Blyth. Reprinted with the permission of The Hokuseido Press, Tokyo. "Ha! the butterfly—" from *Japanese Lyrics* by Lafcadio Hearn. Reprinted with the permission of Houghton Mifflin Company. "The nightingales—" from *The Pepper Pod* by Kenneth Yasuda. Reprinted with the permission of Alfred A. Knopf, Inc. "Come on, Owl—" from *The Autumn Wind* by Lewis Mackenzie, Wisdom of the East Series. Reprinted with the permission of John Murray, Ltd., London. "A drop of rain—" from *The Year of My Life* by Nobuyuki Yuasa. Reprinted with the permission of the University of California Press.

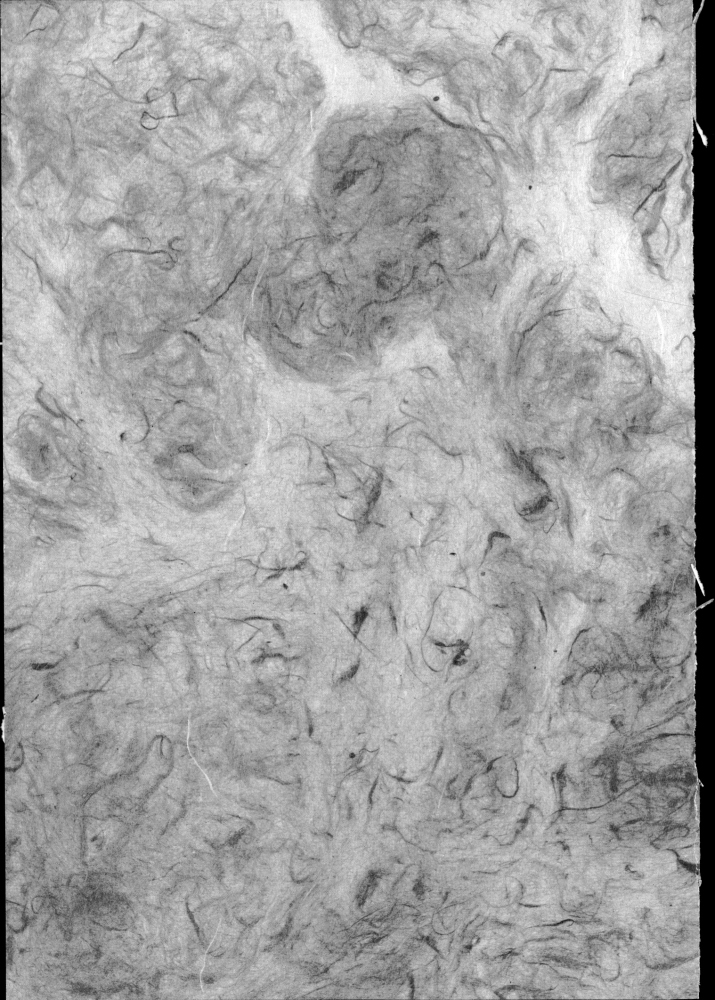